When the Street Lights Come on

By
Lori B. Rouse

I WOULD LIKE TO DEDICATE THIS BOOK TO MY GRANDCHILDREN. AS YOU GROW, MAY YOUR SUMMERS BE AS ADVENTUROUS AND EXCITING AS MINE WERE.

This morning as my feet stretch down to the floor,
I put on my clothes and run to the door;
To see the sun rise, no clouds in the sky,
It is time to start playing with my friends nearby!

I begin my chores quickly and when they're all done,
Out the door I go, now it's time for my fun;
It's early in the day so I have time to spare,
Thinking of fun in the summertime air.

I call all my friends on our telephone,
Our goal for the day is to be on our own;
The day seems long and unexpected sometimes,
We experience fun that will last a lifetime.

There's a short walk to the end of my street,
At the neighbor's house is where we'll all meet;
Seeing one another at the beginning of the day,
Makes life in the neighborhood worth the stay.

We say our hellos, as all friends do,
We talk and we laugh, and tell a joke or two!
Our day will take us to unknown places,
We face each adventure as if they are races.

We find ourselves walking near a small stream
out back,
 Walking in water like we're part of a pack;
We spend time kicking up water with our feet,
We splash and we splash until we are beat.

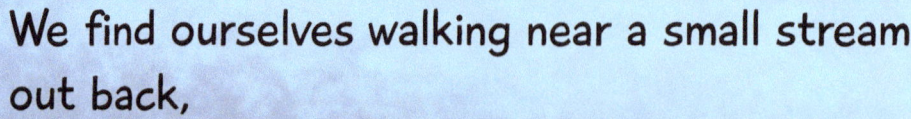

As we are playing and splashing water around,
Tadpoles are dancing without a sound;
We catch a few with our hands pressed together,
They swim very fast and are as light as a feather.

Oh, this is so fun, but we must move on,
If we do not hurry, our day will be gone;
Time is important when playing with friends,
There is much to do before the day ends.

Well, out of the stream and back on the land,
Our day is not over because we now have a plan!
Our next fun adventure is to ride bikes downhill;
With no hands and no feet, it takes a lot of skill.

Now we're riding downhill in a race with great speed,
Hands off the handlebars and taking the lead;
Eating bugs, getting stung while moving so fast,
Accidents do happen, but it's still a blast.

Our bikes are ten-speed, all shiny and new,
Squeezing the breaks until our hands are blue;
We depend on these bikes to carry us miles,
Racing each other gives us all smiles.

Moving on, still playing, it's early in the day,
Another idea must be thought of so we can stay;
At last, we find, more friends to invite,
It's time to play baseball, while it's still light.

Our neighbor's yard is the place
where we play,
We get permission, so our moms
let us stay;
All the bases are laid and real
equipment is used,
Teams are divided and those
without skills, are excused.

Our baseball teams are interesting to watch,
We have all the equipment to be topnotch;
Each inning we play, we give it our all,
All the rules are enforced when we yell "Play Ball."

No umpire is needed, we call our own game,
When bad calls are made, someone is to blame;
Sometimes we fuss, sometimes we fight,
This happens when the game is not played just right.

When the game is over, we go our own way,
To find some more fun to complete our day;
The sun is quickly moving near the west,
We must hurry, you must have guessed.

Now, it's up in the air, we must go,
Climbing tall trees with their branches real low;
A scrape, and a bruise, we sometime can get,
We play very hard and try not to fret.

We pick low branches to try a new trick,
Hanging upside down and moving real quick;
Releasing our hands from the branch like we're grown
If we are lucky, not one broken bone.

Our day ends well with many hours of play,
But I know the hour I must quit, the exact time of day;
My mom says, "Come home" when the street lights
come on,
All the kids in the neighborhood soon will be gone.

That light has a meaning that a watch doesn't share,
The meaning of the street light is now very rare;
I say good-bye to my friends that are near,
I'll see you tomorrow, the fun will be here!

THE END